A Season of Disruption

A Season of Disruption

A Season Of Disruption

Jacqueline P. Walker

Writings By Jackie

ACKNOWLEDGMENTS

This work is a fictional depiction of real-life experiences. I changed names, dates, places, and some elements of the actual events. I am grateful to those who supported this labor of love, producing a piece that I hope will resonate with and inspire others.

DEDICATION

Nothing compares with the strength, determination, and perseverance of a mother's love!

Yesterday, I laughed.
Today, I cry.
What will tomorrow bring?
Yesterday was filled with joy,
hopes, and dreams soon to be fulfilled.
Today there is pain and dissatisfaction,
failure and losses abound.
Yesterday, I climbed to the mountaintop.
Today, I tumble to the valley below.
But tomorrow, I must begin my climb again UPWARD.
Remembering yesterday and today.
Recapturing hopes and dreams.
Never repeating failures.
Laying down burdens.
Finding a pot of gold.
Sharing experiences.
Creating a future from the past and the present.
Realizing that life is a mixture of:
good and bad,
winning and losing,
ups and downs,
yesterday and today,
Believing that there will come a TOMORROW.

WHERE DO I BEGIN?

CHAPTER 1

Disruption is a popular buzzword these days, especially in business. With the ever-increasing advances in technology, disruption does not just happen to us. Instead, it is something we proactively choose. It is a change from the norm. Being disruptive means being innovative, anticipating future needs, and taking a chance by doing things differently to achieve the required results with minimal delays. When we choose to disrupt, we find new ways to maneuver around obstacles that would otherwise thwart our progress.

I was watching TV with my mother a few weeks ago. A news segment highlighted "upstart" companies that took over transportation and home entertainment markets by not merely entering the market with products similar to those already existing but by projecting future needs and creating offerings that resonated with customers. By the time existing companies responded, it was too late: they lost customers and market share, and their businesses failed. The reporter referred to these occurrences as *the theory of business disruption.* After the program ended, Mother thought it was good, but she was not overly impressed.

"There's nothing new and amazing about that," she said. "If you want to win, you never follow what someone else is doing. You do what you have to do based on your drive and inner strength while remaining flexible and open to new ideas. If you can't do that, it will be difficult to find success, and life will become a heavy load."

I thought about it, and then I had to acknowledge

that she was *oh so right*. Precisely fifty years ago, that is what happened to us. My mother, my siblings, and I faced disruption. We did not expect it, but we stepped right into it because we quickly realized that if we were not merely to survive but thrive, we had to take charge of the unexpected events that threatened to derail our hopes and dreams. It was a season filled with significant changes: death, physical separation, emotional stress, and financial challenge, but we were unwilling to succumb to those forces. We learned quickly to find a way around these obstacles so they would not control our lives, steal our hopes, and crush our dreams. No, sir, as David did with Goliath, we were bold enough to point our slingshots squarely at the spot between the eyes of disruption and courageously aim. We did not intend to stand around and get run over. My parents had grand plans for our success, and each of us had our own ideas for our future. Our mother and father encouraged us to be confident, determined, strong-willed, courageous, supportive of each other, committed to each other, and bonded in love. We were not going to let anything come against those values. If anyone or anything tried to disrupt our future, we were up to the test to withstand it and stomp it out with all our strength.

I remember the day this challenging season began in our family—the day disruption knocked at our door. It was 1970 in Kingston, Jamaica. A small island in the Caribbean Sea, Jamaica was still growing after gaining its independence a mere eight years earlier. New communities were popping up, and families were buying or building houses to create stability and define legacies. The economy was growing from tourism, manufacturing, and the flourishing bauxite (a natural rock used in many aluminum products) industry. Political and social uprisings were minimal because the economy was stable, and generally, many families were satisfied with their ability not merely to survive but to live a comfortable life. Also, there were not many incidences of government and legal corruption or abuse.

We lived in a housing development that was less

than ten years old. When we moved there five years earlier, there were no schools and supermarkets (just in-home stores run by a few private residents with minimal supplies). We had a variety of vegetables and fruits that grew in our backyard (mango, lime, callaloo, banana, coconut), and we even had a chicken coop from which we gathered fresh eggs. Our daily routines were not extraordinary. We went to school, performed our assigned chores, played in the yard, and attended church every Sunday morning. Life was excellent. As they say on the island, "No problem, man!"

Up to that point in my life, I had no problems. But early one Sunday morning in March 1970, disruption came along to challenge our routine. About four months after my eighth birthday, my family experienced unforeseen changes that would shape our future.

That morning, I got out of bed as I heard the rooster crow. Like most Sunday mornings, the neighborhood was quiet. Sundays were indeed a day of rest. Most people slept in and ventured out only for church services. Since everyone was typically asleep or inside their houses, the rooster's crow was loud and clear as it was the only sound that traveled from outside to inside.

But this morning inside our house seemed eerily quiet. I did not think that I was the only one up, although the others may have slept in since we did not expect to go to church as we usually did. Mother had spent most of the previous day and all night at the hospital because Daddy had been admitted after being hit by a motorcycle. Before Mother had left for the hospital that evening, she told us she did

not know what time she would be home. So, we were unsure of whether we would attend church on Sunday morning. Mother's reluctance to give us a specific time that she would be home should have set off an alarm with us, but we were kids, and up until then, our lives had been happy and routine, so we never expected anything "bad" to happen.

I heard voices in the carport, so I walked through the kitchen and headed in that direction. I saw my brothers, Champ and Kamere, but I did not need them. I was looking for my sister Faith, because I was getting hungry, and my sisters usually saw to my every need when Mother was not around. I turned around to head back inside. I knew Hope (my eldest sister's nickname) was not home (she accompanied Mother on her trip to the hospital), but where in the world was Faith? I don't know why I was surprised, because she always moved to the beat of her own drums. I walked through the living room toward the front of the house. That's when I heard it: a car pulling up to our home and screams breaking the silence. Well, I'd found one of my sisters, and it wasn't Faith. It was Hope—my parents' firstborn. "He's dead. He's dead!" she moaned and hollered all at the same time.

I remember my body shaking, and I suddenly felt cold; my head started pounding at the same time, and I couldn't fully understand what she was saying, although I heard her loud and clear. Instinctively all my eight-year-old self knew to do at that moment was cry. And that is what I did. As the tears streamed down my face, I ran toward the front door. I opened the door just as my uncle's car pulled up into the carport. My mother, Murna, and my sister Hope exited—both sobbing in sadness. By then, my eyes were overflowing with tears, and my head was spinning. I didn't know what to say or what to do. I remember Hope hugging me, and then I saw Champ, Kamere, and Faith coming from inside the house to see what was going on.

I thought it was a dream. It seemed like a bad dream, and I wanted to wake up from it. But sadly, it was not. I'd heard what my sister screamed from the car, so I knew it was official. Daddy was gone forever. As I think back on that day, I guess, deep down inside, I wasn't surprised when I heard the news. I was deeply saddened. I didn't want it to be accurate, but honestly, I wasn't totally surprised because, secretly, I'd just had this feeling. When Mother left us to go to the hospital, there was a strange and distant look in her eyes. As much as she tried to stay calm and not reveal the severity of the situation, somehow, I sensed something unsettling that I did not understand at the time.

So, how did we get here, to this harrowing Sunday morning? This startling event began on Saturday. The day started like any other Saturday. Hope headed off early with her friends; she had a sporting event at school. As was customary before heading out, Hope said goodbye to Daddy. I'll never forget that morning. Hope was wearing a red-and-white culotte outfit with a bow at the right hip that our grandmother, who we lovingly called "Auntie Mattie," sent from New Jersey. Hope was in high school and extremely particular about style and fashion.

Daddy looked at her as she greeted him and critiqued her outfit, saying, "It's a little cool out. Do you think you can survive in that?"

"Yes, Daddy!" Hope answered, bobbing her head up and down to convince him because she really wanted to wear the outfit.

"Okay, then," was his short response, shrugging his shoulder.

"Bye, Daddy," Hope answered, never knowing this would be the very last exchange she would ever have with her father.

11

Daddy had breakfast and headed into town. Our mother was scurrying around cleaning. My brothers were halfway doing their chores and halfway playing. Faith was begrudgingly doing her chores (as usual, wondering why she was holding down the fort for the rest of us kids). I was basking in the glory of being the youngest child and not having to do chores like my older siblings. Instead, I found a book to read. I had tons of books; reading was my favorite pastime.

Morning turned to afternoon, uneventful until our neighbor came running up the driveway looking harried and loudly calling, "Murna, Murna!" Mother stepped outside, exchanged a few words, and ran with him to his house to take a phone call because we did not have a phone in our home.

She returned, nervous, stuttering, "I have to go. It's your father; there was an accident." My brothers peered at her with serious looks on their faces but never uttered a word. As usual, it was Faith who asked the tough questions. "Exactly what happened, Mother? Is he okay? Is he hurt bad?"

Mother's eyes welled up with tears. She turned her head slightly away as she babbled while rummaging through the drawers, grabbing keys and some papers, "All I know is a motorcycle hit him as he was crossing the street, Main Street, and they took him by ambulance to the hospital. I have to go now. Please stay inside. Your sister should be home soon."

"Is that all you know?" quizzed Faith, slightly indignant.

"*F-a-i-t-h*," Mother slowly said, "Let me leave so I can go to find out more and make sure he gets the care he needs." Mother was definitely in a hurry and avoided eye contact.

"Okay," Faith replied curtly, folding her arms and slowly walking away although still clearly annoyed.

Mother, likely noticing Faith's stance and tone, took a deep breath as if to gain strength and looked at her daughter lovingly, wanting to go after her. But as she heard a car's horn blowing, Mother grabbed her purse and ran out of the house. My uncle, who lived across the street and two doors down, was ready to take her to the hospital. I remained quiet. I did not ask Mother any questions, and I did not bother Faith. I just went back to my books, half reading and half thinking about what I had heard, the words, the tone and urgency of Mother's voice, the look on her face and in her eyes. I knew Faith did not have any more information than I did, so there was no point in peppering her with questions. That is how I've always thought things out. There was no point in asking questions when I knew we both heard and saw the same things. I went back to reading because I could always find solace in stories to calm my fears and quiet anxiety.

When Hope arrived, we told her everything we knew, how Mother got a phone call and rushed off to the hospital.

"Ah, it's probably no big deal. Daddy will be fine. Remember a few years back when he had to handle a commotion at work, and somebody tried to hit him over the head, missed, and tore his shoulder apart?"

"Yeah, on Boxing Day," I interjected.

"You would know the exact day," replied Faith, looking at me annoyed.

"Right, and that didn't turn out to be anything real serious—he didn't die, and he didn't stay in the hospital for more than a day or two. So, I don't care what you heard. Just like when they tried to hit him over the head, and the hit landed on his shoulder, I'm betting if the motorcycle did hit him, it wasn't going fast, and maybe he just hurt a leg or something, and he'll be okay. Yes, he'll be home before you know it," said Hope with confidence. "Where was he when it happened, anyway?"

"He was in town on Main Street. When he left out this morning, I heard him tell Mother he would stop in to see Aunt Edna because, you know, she is always at her store on Main Street on Saturdays. Then he said that he was going to Macon's Pharmacy across the street from Aunt Edna's to get some ointment to rub on his shoulder. I bet that's just where it happened," I blurted out.

Both Faith and Hope stared at me for a second. They didn't say much, but their eye-rolls said it all.

As young as I was, I always knew what was going on, had a lot of information, and had an opinion to share. The older girls were getting tired of their little sister's know-it-all outbursts. They ignored me and continued their exchange.

"Yeah, that shoulder he hurt in the Boxing Day incident because he just so happened to take a step, and luckily it missed the top of his head. That could have turned out awful, and it didn't," replied Faith confidently. "Daddy is tough because outside of having to rub that shoulder every now and then, he just moved right on as though nothing happened. But I pray the hit from the motorcycle didn't break any bones. I bet he'll be fine this time too. Daddy always is! I won't worry because I know he'll be fine."

"Exactly, Faith, he didn't die from that hit on his shoulder! And he's been walking around as though it's business as usual. I know my daddy; he will be fine. I don't care what hit him. Daddy can make it through anything," was Hope's unwavering response, getting in the last word as always.

Again, I picked up a book as I always did when I

felt nervous or uncertain. Champ and Kamere never chimed in on the conversation and simply walked away after Hope's last declaration. I don't know if they believed it. I'm not sure that I believed it myself. But if my sisters believed it, then I thought I ought to believe it. And since Faith and Hope were united in their belief, I was also willing to believe, and that's what I tried to do.

Later that evening, Mother returned. She looked sad, and her eyes were red. She tried not to cry and to remain upbeat, but we could tell it was serious and not a minor incident. Hope asserted her position as the eldest child, asking what exactly happened and how he was. She was not going to accept Mother brushing her off.

"Okay," Mother relented, "a motorcycle hit him as he was crossing the street. He hit his head on the curb. They rushed him, unconscious, to the hospital. He was still unconscious when I left the hospital."

Wow, now I saw a change in Hope and Faith's demeanors. They didn't speak it out loud, but as I perceived, the seriousness of the situation had hit them squarely in the face. The fantasy of *super* Daddy who could withstand any blow was no more. Faith walked away. She was never much for showing her feelings in public (even to us). Hope, being Hope, wanted the facts. She wanted eyewitness confirmation, not hearsay, even if it was from her own mother.

But Mother didn't appear to be up to saying much more. She came home for a few hours to see about us; after all, mothering is what she did best. She intended to feed us and get us settled for bed before returning to the hospital.

"I'm going with you," Hope said firmly.

"No," Mother replied, "stay here with the others."

"Absolutely not," Hope responded, "I'm going."

Hope was stubborn, and Mother was not up to a fight, so Hope won.

The next time we heard from them was the bellow and scream of Hope on Sunday morning as the car pulled up. This normally calm, cool, and collected teenager lost her composure. It was clear that Hope was shaken and maybe even scared. Before that morning, I didn't recall ever seeing my big sister so worked up, unsettled, and out of control. The seemingly unthinkable had happened; her daddy had died! Hope was losing it, and at that moment, I didn't quite know what to expect or what would happen from that day forward.

It seemed that within minutes everyone had heard the news because before we knew it, the neighbors were swarming our house. I felt overwhelmed by all the attention, since I was the quiet one who was always uncomfortable interacting with others. I typically waved quickly in reply to a neighborly hello and ran inside to my parents and siblings—my comfort zone. I had a couple of select friends; otherwise, my attention focused on reading my stories. I didn't like anyone asking me questions or fussing over me. Somehow it all felt intrusive. My parents and siblings were the centers of my world, and I limited any other relationship's scope. There was a line in the sand, and I was not too fond of when anyone tried to cross it, even when they had good intentions. This swarm of people wanting to hug me felt suffocating, but I did not want to be rude. I did my best to display courtesy and manners. Then just when fear and sadness, combined with the stifling crowd, were about to take hold of me, I felt a tug on my sleeve. I looked to my left, and it was Faith.

"Come on," she said, "let's go out back and play."

"Play?" I asked as we walked away.

I was confused as she pulled me by the arm. *Daddy is dead, and Faith wants to play?*

"Yes, play. What don't you get about that?" Faith asked indignantly.

"Daddy is dead, Faith; I don't think we should be playing," I answered. "Do you really feel like playing? I mean, aren't you sad or upset or anything?" I continued, trembling as tears ran down my cheeks.

She sighed, stared at me, and shook her head before speaking. "I know Daddy is dead," she replied with an attitude. "Of course I'm sad. We're never going to see him, hug him, talk to him, go places, do stuff, smile, or laugh with him ever again. But I know my daddy; he only wants us to live as he taught us.

He wants us to be strong like he told us to be. He doesn't want us sitting around, crying, and giving up."

I stared at her, unresponsive and wondering what was wrong with her. At that moment, I didn't understand Faith wanting to play when Daddy was dead. Mother was painfully sad (I'd never seen her look this way before), and Hope was freaking out.

"Do you think if you sit around and cry all day, he'll come back to life? Do you think if you just stay sad, that will make him smile again?" she responded quizzically.

"Nope," I whispered.

"Okay, then let's play," she said.

"All right," I said, since I had no real comeback for her assertions, and when I thought about it, like her, I knew my daddy and what he had taught us. Everything Faith said sounded like something he would have said. I needed to hear it and always felt somehow Daddy had something to do with Faith's tongue lashing that day.

We walked to the backyard, escaping the crowd

and playing until our mother sent Hope to find us. As I reflect now, that exchange was therapy, and I am happy we played instead of letting sadness overtake us. Faith and her never-stress personality stopped me from wallowing and getting absorbed by the enormity of the situation. Her innocent wisdom allowed me to be what I was—an eight-year-old girl with dreams and desires that were beginning to take root, even though my daddy's time in my life had come to an end.

THE FAMILY GENESIS

CHAPTER 2

Our parents were not your typical couple. No, they did not fit seamlessly into the compatibility formula that many of us hold dear. But somehow, they ended up together.

Born Victor Claude Moreland, Daddy was a career man with supervisory responsibilities. Our father was sixteen years older than our mother. But our mother had him in height by four to five inches. (Their wedding picture with Mother standing street level and Daddy standing three steps up was always a source of laughter for us kids!) They were born and raised on different sides of the island, but both landed in Kingston, where they met. Daddy was hardworking, opinionated, arrogant, and loved being in charge.

My father was the middle child of the children born from my grandfather's second marriage after his first wife's death, and the children from that first union were adults. Daddy was raised as much by his parents as by a sister from his father's first marriage. The Morelands were a close-knit family, and their heritage and legacy included land in the beautiful terrain of Brentmoor Hills. As a matter of fact, my father's grave lies in a family cemetery there. He was laid to rest at the foot of his sister's grave (the one who raised him) and not far from his father's grave. My grandfather's grave lies in between the graves of his two wives. We chuckle about that from time to time. But we remember the lush greenery of Brentmoor Hills and the many streams and rivers that ran through it. One even ran through the family cemetery.

Mother was a stay-at-home mom and housewife with little to no formal work experience or career training. She worked all her life unless you exclude the years when she was a housewife and caretaker. As a child, she grew up working on her father's farm from dawn to dusk, delivering milk across the countryside, and completing any additional chores required. Mother is (she is alive and well) super hardworking, meek, mild, determined, and kind.

We have always said, "Mother," and never "Mom." I am not quite sure why, except that was what felt comfortable to us. I guess that is normal for us because when it comes to names or how we refer to each other in our family, we expect the unexpected. There has been a constant issue throughout our family of names being twisted, added, or changed outside of the official realms. I like to refer to it as *the dysfunction of names.* Please note that phrase because you will quickly understand its meaning and significance in our family as you continue reading.

Most everyone calls my mother Murna, although she was born Julia Anne Wiles. Her mother, Julia Anne, named her firstborn as she was named and had that name officially placed on her birth certificate. In those days in Jamaica, registering a child's name on a birth certificate did not require the parent's signature. In fact, the parents or their designee would take paperwork from the hospital to the registrar's office with the name they wanted on the birth certificate. The registrar would write the information by hand into the official registration journal as well as write it on a form that they gave to parents or their designee. Auntie Mattie (how we referred to our grandmother) registered our mother as Julia Anne.

Her father wanted no part of that name and did not care what they had in the registrar's office. He called her what he liked, Murna. But he took it even further. He told everyone that was her name and asked everyone to call her Murna. My grandmother did not resist, complain, or defy him, but she also never changed that official birth certificate. Growing up, Mother knew no other name. After accepting our father's proposal, she needed to produce her birth certificate to acquire a marriage license, which prompted my grandmother to break the news to Mother that her name was not Murna. Murna was a pseudonym. Mother tells us she was surprised, but there was nothing she could do but accept it. "Murna" had grown on her, so she never stopped using it, and others have never stopped using it. She only uses Julia on official documents and in professional work settings. Otherwise, everyone else, even my grandmother (up to her death), uses Murna. Still, now and then, I take the opportunity to teasingly call her Julia or sometimes Julie, whichever rolls off my tongue. I am her youngest child, so it's not done in disrespect. It's just a loving daughter-mother ribbing about her phantom name.

It was only after my grandmother's passing that several close family members realized that my grandmother's name was Julia Anne and that my mother's name was also Julia Anne. Before my grandmother's death, most of the family only knew her as Mattie, and they knew my mother as Murna. They were stunned to find out their real names and that they shared the name Julia Anne.

My sisters and I had a good laugh about that as one family member looked at Mother questioningly and said, "That's different. You're a junior?"

By now, you should have a good understanding of the dysfunction of names, right? I hope so, because it ain't over!

Let me tell you more. For instance, if you are wondering why we call our grandmother (whose real name is Julia Anne) Auntie Mattie, well, that was all Hope's doing. My sister Hope is our grandma's first grandchild, and when she visited the family, every other child was one of my grandma's nieces or nephews, and they called her Auntie Mattie. Hope did not want to be the only child who had to call her Grandma. Why? Well, she told me she just liked the sound of "Auntie Mattie" better than the sound of "Grandma."

So, Hope called our grandma, Auntie Mattie, to the chagrin of others, who complained and asked my grandma to stop Hope from calling her Auntie. But our grandma was always the most easygoing, no-stress lady, and as she recounted the story for me years ago, she said, "I told them if she wants to call me Auntie Mattie, let her!" Hope never stopped, and as you will learn, Hope always set the pace for the rest of us. As a result, we all called our grandma, Auntie Mattie.

And as for how the name Mattie came to be (since that is not her birth name), it remains a mystery. Frankly, in all the years I chatted with my grandmother, I never asked. I know that seems strange, but remember I said the dysfunction of names was a frequent occurrence in my family. As such, I was not particularly curious about it. I wrote it off as another one of those off-the-cuff name changes. Indeed, as I reflect on it, as a child, I thought Mattie was short for Matilda (I heard many adults call her by that name too). Then as I grew up, I found out that was not her name. Mother doesn't know the origins of the Mattie-Matilda name. I have asked others, but no one knows. They just heard it their entire life and assumed it was her given name, so they used it. And even when they learned otherwise, they never stopped calling her Mattie. There is even more to come on the dysfunction of names, which has been a deep-rooted cycle in our family that was difficult to break.

Nevertheless, let's get back to the *real* story and learn more about my family and our lives after Daddy's death. As the family leader, Daddy set the rules of engagement for the family. Mother enforced them. Our mother made sure we did our chores, completed our homework, and came home (unless there was a good reason) before Daddy got home. He often required a head count as soon as he arrived. Daddy was not much for us having friends and hanging around the neighborhood.

"Plant yourselves in the backyard," he would say. "I made five of you; play with each other."

I guess it was not all bad; it made us grow remarkably close, and nothing has ever been able to break the ties that bind us.

Hope, Tina Irene Moreland, is the eldest, strong-willed, intelligent, well-spoken, a born leader, and just as opinionated and self-assured as her father. Before she hit puberty, Daddy had her doing trigonometry and calculus. She was his "Hope"—a unique child on whom he placed high expectations for the future. Daddy never used her given name—Tina. He called her Hope, and we do too. However, unlike our mother, Hope has always known that her given name is Tina. She used it at school, and she uses it in her business and professional life. But to those near and dear to her, it is Hope, and she would not have it any other way. It is still odd whenever I must refer to her by her given name. It is as though I am talking about a stranger rather than my beloved sister, Hope.

Before Hope could choose a profession, one was selected for her by her daddy. He commanded all children and adults (except her siblings and Mother) to refer to her as Doctor Hope. Adults loved Hope for her manners, smarts, and eloquence. Her brothers and sisters revered her as our leader and our accomplished eldest sister, who always seemed to get it right! Throughout the rest of the family, every teenager and child hated her because they were often compared to her but could never measure up. It wasn't Hope's fault; she was not arrogant, insincere, or mean.

On the contrary, she was—and still is—a caretaker of sorts, always looking out for others. A social butterfly by nature, she always had a slew of friends and acquaintances in her circle. Without a doubt, wherever she goes, she is "that girl"—the person everyone else wants to know. Still, she always toed the line by being careful of what she did and with whom. Hope was not typically one to rebel against her father's direction or wishes. No, her priority was to make him proud, and she continues to do so.

Then there is Regal William Moreland, the second born and the eldest son, an athletic young man with a likable personality and adventurous spirit who enjoys every minute of life. We called him Champ because he was consistently winning at his athletic pursuits. Without a doubt, if we took a vote on the most likely to break Daddy's rules, Champ would win by a landslide! He was not a bad kid, and he was not a troubled kid. He was simply a free-spirited young man with a zest for life who was more interested in having fun than being tied to books or chores. He was athletic and loved sports, particularly track and field and soccer. He took every opportunity to sneak off to play soccer or some other sport with the neighborhood boys, knowing that there would be consequences for going off without permission but willing to live dangerously, despite having a good idea of what the punishment would entail. He pushed curfews to the limit, coming home at the last second most of the time. On several occasions, Mother went looking for him to coax him back home before Daddy's arrival. Just imagine a twelve-year-old boy running and juking his mother as if he were controlling and maneuvering a soccer ball around an opponent. Then there was Mother (who was certainly not dressed for the challenge) trying to keep up and corral him (with no success) while every other young man at the park laughed and cheered Champ on as he made her look like an unworthy opponent. It was memorable; you had to be there to appreciate it! He is still the same free-willed, lovable man today.

Faith is the middle child. A loner, she has always stayed close to her family instead of developing a network of friends. She is stubborn, carefree, and willing to buck the system and speak her mind. Her name defines her behavior, reflecting her confidence and trust that things would always work out for her good. She was never one to worry or get anxious. Now, "Faith" is a given name, but like the other women in the family, there is a story behind her full name. Her formal and official name *was* Corrine Faith Moreland, or so we thought. At home, we called her Faith (and still do). But at school and for everyone outside the family, it *was* Corrine. I stress it *was* because her name had to change unexpectedly.

Shortly after Daddy's passing, Mother rounded up our birth certificates. She wanted to get a passport for each of us as she pondered the family's options, including potentially migrating to the US. It came to her attention that there was a new issue or format of birth certificates, and she needed to get updated versions. When she made the trip to the registrar's office, there was one problem. They insisted that the paperwork on file listed Faith's name as "Corrie" and not "Corrine." But on Mother's copy of the birth certificate, it stated "Corrine." There was a discrepancy.

The registrar's office gave Mother a choice to leave it as they had it on file, "Corrie," or go through some long, convoluted process for a name change. Mother came home and called us together; she laid out the options and the obstacles.

Once again, in her matter-of-fact style, Faith said, "I'll keep Corrie as long as we pronounce it Kôrē and not Korī."

We agreed to support her wishes (and to this day, we have without wavering). Mother changed her name at school, and we changed it throughout the neighborhood and our network of friends. I do not know what Mother told the school. When anyone in our community asked why Faith's name changed, we simply gave the *Moreland look*, which meant we didn't feel the need to talk about it. We had that reputation throughout the neighborhood, courtesy of Daddy (some things are just our family stuff, and we didn't need to give explanations). They didn't bother us about it; they just obliged. We never used the name Corrine again within our family, and we have adamantly corrected anyone who mispronounced

Corrie. I bet you clearly see the confusion and complication names have wrought in my family; again, the dysfunction of names.

Even as a child, Faith said what she meant and meant what she said. Her responses and comments were never insolent or disrespectful, but they were always so insightful and compelling that they forced you to look at the person in the mirror. Often her feedback left me feeling guilty or shortsighted, forcing me to rethink my strategy or choices. Even now, we call her *the voice of reason* because she has a way of settling an argument by saying something that makes us all feel sometimes silly, sometimes petty, and occasionally selfish. Faith is probably the most diligent of us all. I remember when I was finally assigned chores, she helped me or completed them on my behalf to keep me out of trouble. (I couldn't seem to get them done because my priority remained getting back to reading books as quickly as possible). She had natural athletic abilities but no interest in pursuing them.

She just wanted to be a little girl with no pressure

or demand to live out her parents' dreams. She had desires and planned to pursue them whatever they were, regardless of whether others thought they were foolish or frivolous. Even as a child, Faith understood that some things in this life were out of your control, and you just had to believe and keep striving to get to your goal. With her, there was no time for crying over things you could not change. As I think about it, she was a little girl living by the Serenity Prayer: accepting the things she could not change, changing the things she could, and wise enough to understand the difference.

Kamere Victor Moreland (Kam) is the youngest son. He is mild-mannered and soft-spoken like his mother but reflects the quest for excellence and leadership instilled by his father. You are never quite sure what you will get from Kamere. One minute he is the introvert in the corner alone. Then the next, he is the jokester, ensuring he is the center of attention. And then the next, the workaholic, can do any type of job you ask, especially if it involves guiding and directing others' work. He has a chameleon's attributes, changing to be what he needs to be when he needs to be it. Or maybe there is an ongoing tug-of-war within him to choose if he would prefer just to be left alone or if he wants to be a part of the social scene. Regardless, the driving force within him is to excel at any and every opportunity. He subscribes to the belief that failure is not an option. Yet his playful persona puts people at ease quickly, and once there is a connection, he immediately flips from introvert to extrovert without blinking an eye. If he likes you, he loves you; but an extensive process is required to get to where he loves you. Kamere wants what he wants and is not usually willing to settle for less. But he understands that he must earn things and so diligently works to acquire his heart's desires.

Then there is me, Sasha, the youngest. As an avid reader, I would describe myself as curious (always trying to learn), much more of a writer than a talker, and someone who treasures solitude but appreciates creativity and the arts. Quiet and introspective, I don't usually say much, but when I have something to say, I say it with vigor. Also, when I care about something or someone, my loyalty, covering, and support are passionate, to say the least. Moreover, when I know I am right on any topic, I will stand my ground and never be moved. I guess that is why I have often been lovingly accused of being competitive. I like to think that I simply love being the best I can be and giving the best that I have. Whatever the assignment, I strive to excel.

Books were my best friend. I looked forward to Saturday afternoon outings to the bookmobile. Faith and Kamere would accompany me, but most of the time, I was the only one who left with books. For Faith and Kamere, it was more of a social event to see and interact with friends or classmates. After every trip to the bookmobile, I struggled home with a stack of books while they skipped, danced, and chatted all the way home. After our first venture to the bookmobile, neither Kamere nor Faith were inclined to offer help carrying my books. They were not unkind, but I threw a tantrum that first week because I didn't particularly appreciate how they tossed my books around, accidentally dropping them or snuggled them under their underarm during the trip home. My books are treasured possessions, and I handle them as such. After my first experience witnessing how they carried my books, I refused their help. Of course, Faith was not offended.

"Let her struggle with her books by herself, since that makes her happy," she advised Kamere each time he tried to assist me.

And, after getting one of my stern glances, Kamere would acquiesce and follow Faith's recommendation. I didn't mind, and I wasn't angry, because I didn't want anyone mishandling my prized possessions.

My reading interests covered various subjects and topics. I started out reading young adult mysteries and English classics. Then I graduated to poems, short stories and full-length biographies or novels from a host of African American authors who reinforced what my father always told me; I was as brilliant, capable, and gifted as anyone else. I remember spending many hours alone indoors reading, until Faith commanded me to come out and play because they needed another body to fill out teams. Never much of a complainer, I would do it despite my lack of athletic prowess.

Songs, both the music and lyrics, are my next love outside of books. I don't play an instrument, and I certainly have no vocal talent. Still, I enjoy musical beats and inspiring, thought-provoking, memory jogging, and just fun, lyrical content. Earlier, I noted that we didn't have a telephone at home during this season of our life. Well, we didn't have television either. But we did have a radio and record player. Daddy bought a Grundig stereo. We heard it came from Germany and was supposed to be the best. I remember it looked like a piece of furniture. It was encased in a polished, dark-brown wood cabinet. One of my first assigned chores was to dust the cabinet from week to week to keep it shiny. Of course, Faith had to help me out as somehow that seemed to be challenging for me. Admittedly, chores were never my strength.

By the way, my given name is Sasha Martina Moreland, and it still stands. Finally, we broke the cycle of the dysfunction of names. Every now and then, one of my siblings will refer to me as Sash. But that is the extent of a valid nickname, pet name, or name change for me. Although sometimes my sister refers to me as "the Little Hurricane." Reportedly, days before I was born, Hurricane Hattie originated in the Caribbean Sea. On the day I was born, the storm was swirling in the Atlantic Ocean, having reached Category 5 status, and many feared it would make landfall in Jamaica. Fortunately for Jamaica, it did not make a direct hit (just a lot of rain). Unfortunately, it made landfall in Belize, causing significant damage (and I am sure that remains a sad memory for that island, so I am certainly not making light of it). But my sister's perspective is that what I earlier referred to as vigor and passion for standing my ground and supporting causes and people are a little more intense than I let on. Therefore, when I get started, she quips, "There goes the Little Hurricane."

While I am acknowledging nicknames, I might as well reveal another little-known one I earned when I was still in primary (elementary) school in Jamaica. For a short time, a few schoolmates took to calling me Likkle Yōot (Little Youth). The origination of the name was twofold. First, I was one of the smallest children in a group that walked to school and back home daily. During these trips, we chatted about events in our families, the neighborhood, or school. As we talked, I had a way of disputing and rebuffing many of the group's recollections of people, events, and the details of specific encounters. I could recall events no one else seemed to be able to and would confidently tell others their information was wrong (I have this problem at home too, Little Hurricane).

During one discussion amongst the group of kids that walked to school together, an older and taller boy said in Jamaican dialect, "Wī de likkle Yōot tink she nō so much?" (Why does the little youth think that she knows so much?) Of course, I was irritated at the name-calling and walked away, as it reminded me of my siblings' exasperating looks or comments whenever I corrected them about family events. Well, the name stuck with my classmates for about a year or so. I was so happy when they got tired of saying it and moved on to something else.

We, the Moreland siblings, run the gamut in personality and desires. Still, the things we all have in common are the willingness to work hard, the quest for independence and success, and uncontested loyalty to each other, our mother, and our daddy.

I remember as soon as Daddy pulled his car into the driveway in the evenings, Mother quickly set out his slippers and the newspaper. That would be our cue to wash up for dinner and get to the table. We also had to be prepared for Daddy's question and answer session. The conversation was not just about what you learned in school that day—yes, he included that. But Daddy was more concerned with our future. He wanted us to outline our plans. We never knew when he would call on us to present our goal statement. Therefore, we (well, most of us) were always prepared to pitch a high-level summary of our future career path.

Hope would say, "I'm going to be a doctor, Daddy."

As for Champ, his comment was, "I'm going to learn to work on cars and engines just like you,

Daddy."

Kamere had his plan, "I'm going to knock buildings down and create new ones."

I always had the same response, "I'm going to be a teacher, Daddy."

Of course, there was one outlier, Faith. She never had a career pitch. She stuck to her "I do what I want to" mindset. Each time she said, "I think I'll just be a lady looking good and living life in the hustle and bustle of the city, like the ones I see on King Street." King Street was one of the busiest streets in the downtown business districts where most people who held office jobs worked. We knew that was not what Daddy wanted to hear.

As you heard, most of us always had a great career choice picked out and would say it to Daddy with enthusiasm. In contrast, our darling Faith's response never gave Daddy the reassurance he needed that she had the types of goals or plans he expected of her. Whenever it was time for this family ritual, the rest of us would cringe as Faith's turn rolled around because we knew what to expect. She would not budge. Admittedly though, we also knew well enough that she was the most honest of the bunch. At that age, she had no idea what career she would pursue, and she was not going to fake it to please her father. The rest of us opted for the easy way out to appease him. Still, we laugh about it now because we acknowledge that although we were often uncomfortable making this presentation, it was a good exercise that added to our growth and development. As we matured, we realized that it was not necessarily about sticking with the exact area of pursuit you spoke about as a child; it was about learning to set goals.

School and academic achievements were a critical part of Daddy's rules. A report card with a bad grade was not acceptable and came with consequences. I am not saying there was never a bad grade from the five of us. If that happened and Daddy found out, you had to be prepared to explain and deal with his defined consequences. On the other hand, if you did well, he would announce it far and wide, constantly praising you and adamantly bragging about your accomplishments to anyone he could.

Daddy also had his way of challenging us academically. Actually, that mainly was Hope. He was convinced that she was going to be successful, and he pushed her. I remember what we refer to as Hope's University story. We've told this story from time to time, and we often get looks of skepticism. But Mother certainly confirmed it. We remember it well because we lived through the intensity of that period.

I don't know if they still do, but in the 1960s, one of the oldest universities in the English-speaking world offered correspondence courses and classes completed through long-distance learning using printed materials sent through the mail. One year, Daddy signed up for a correspondence mathematics (calculus) course through this university. We didn't know until the large envelope came in the mail, and Daddy enacted his plan. See, Daddy had no intention of completing that course. Instead, he assigned Hope to complete every question, every exercise, and every test in the package. After school, Hope's whole focus was on figuring out the answers to complete the course over a one- to two-week period. She worked steadily, and when she finished the package, Daddy asked, "Are you satisfied and confident that you did enough to pass? Don't let me send it in if you're going to fail!" Self-assured and calm, Hope responded with an assertive "Yes. I'm sure, Daddy. I know I passed!"

Daddy packaged the completed materials and mailed them off to the school per the instructions, with his name, Victor Claude Moreland, on every required form. A few months later, another large envelope arrived from the university. The envelope contained a certificate of completion and a congratulatory letter to Victor Claude Moreland for completing the course. Daddy framed that certificate and proudly hung it on the wall. He never hid the truth; instead, he bragged about what his daughter had done. To him, this was a confirmation of her abilities and what she would achieve.

The Moreland children were ecstatic about the news because, despite our ages, we understood enough to recognize what Hope had accomplished. Every time we looked at that certificate, we beamed with pride. It never bothered us that the certificate read *Victor Claude Moreland.* When we looked at it, we saw *Tina Irene Moreland* (Hope). We knew what she had done, and we were and still are so proud of our big sister.

Growing up, we were young and happy. Life as we knew it did not seem bad. We had food to eat and clothes to wear. We played with the neighborhood children and hurried home before Daddy arrived. We played together and entertained ourselves with books, the radio, and records, since television and telephones were luxuries that we could not afford or that Daddy did not deem necessary. Our lack of these technologies did not change our level of happiness or our enthusiasm for life. We continued smiling and living each day as if the best things life had to offer us were yet to come.

We spent a lot of time listening to the radio together or to Mother and Daddy's (mostly Mother's) vinyl recordings. Her musical tastes were somewhat eclectic, ranging from Jamaican ska and reggae artists, English pop-rock, and music from the US covering blues, gospel, country, jazz, and rhythm and blues artists. I often tease her by greeting her singing one of the tunes (usually a blues recording) that Daddy sang to her from time to time.

After dinner and homework, before bedtime, we entertained ourselves with music on the Grundig or radio. Then when Daddy thought it was enough and we had to shut it down, we kids took the broom in hand and held our own family karaoke shows to entertain ourselves. For us, that was great fun. We didn't miss anything because we didn't have a television—that was okay. My memories hold more instances of joy and laughter than sadness and boredom.

Together, we enjoyed trips to the hill country to visit Daddy's relatives. He often sent word well in advance to his family to let them know to expect us. Our mother dressed us in cute outfits, and we prepared for the car ride up the hill, twisting and turning around the bends. More often than not, my mother stuffed the chest area under my clothing with sheets of newspaper. I can imagine the puzzled look on your face, so let me explain. Well, I often got carsick, and for some reason, there was this idea that stuffing my chest and stomach with something firm made it less likely that I would get car sick during the long drive. It worked, or maybe the mere suggestion convinced me to hold it in.

Anyway, we looked forward to arriving at Dearie's, my father's aunt, on each of these trips. She was the best baker I have ever met, so we knew there would be lots of sweet treats for us. Her house sat upon a hill. It didn't have an actual backyard; instead, you ran down the back of the hill and landed at a riverbed. City children like us, who our mother dressed to meet the standard Daddy portrayed to his family, had to take our shoes and socks off to cross the river. We did so willingly, shoes in hand. Dearie always had a few children staying with her whose parents had gone off somewhere (the US maybe) and left them behind for years or, in many cases, forever. They were very well acquainted with the area and the terrain, so they were our guides to explore the river, farmland, and even abandoned houses.

I remember one particular house that we were forbidden to enter. The kids told us it was a haunted house. The owner had died in the home several years before, and no one ever lived there again. It sat there, dilapidated and empty, and who knows what creatures lurked within. The old doors swung open and squeaked as you passed by. I cannot speak for anyone else, but I was certainly scared beyond words just walking past that house. The kids in Dearie's care told us the only way to stay safe from being haunted was to hold hands and chant as we walked by. We believed them. Why not? They lived in the neighborhood, and we did not. As such, we obliged. We held hands, stepped lightly, and chanted as we passed by and probably for another mile just in case. I guess it worked because the ghost never came after me, and I never heard any of my siblings complain of a spirit bothering them.

Those were great times. Sometimes the group of kids caught *janga* (shrimp or crawfish) by hand in the river. I was terrified that they would stick or bite me, so I just watched. I did join in when we picked up fruits like mangoes that fell off the fruit trees or grabbed guineps off the vine. But again, I watched with the others as my adventurous, risk-taking brother Champ climbed the coconut trees and threw coconuts down to us on the ground. Then, of course, there was lunch or dinner or both at Dearie's home. The best part was dessert, bread pudding, or even what many refer to as Jamaican Black cake. We would have some to eat while we were there and some to take home. As a child, it certainly didn't get much better than that. Those days still bring a smile to my face and stir joy in my heart.

As much as we enjoyed the hill country when we visited, we yearned for a bigger adventure. I think we all had big dreams of the US, although I don't recall us saying them out loud to each other. But I know that I thought about it every time I had my nose stuck in one of my many books, and I am sure that thought was not unique to me. Our maternal grandmother, Auntie Mattie, lived in New Jersey. She always sent home the most stylish clothing for us, like the one Hope put on the morning of Daddy's death. My brothers didn't care one way or the other, but my sisters and I were always excited when the box came, by parcel post, to see what pretty dresses or fashionable outfits we would wear that no one else in our neighborhood would ever have. My sisters and I still have a special affinity for pretty dresses. We are always excited about invitations to parties or events, as each occasion is an opportunity to get a new outfit. Of course, we lovingly blame Auntie Mattie for this sweet addiction.

Daddy spent some time in the US working. We thought he would stay, and then we would join him. But he did not. As I recall, he returned home unexpectedly in the middle of the night, banging on the door. We woke up concerned about who was knocking so loudly and with such urgency. For a minute, I thought someone was trying to break in. I remember Champ, fashioning himself *the man of the house*, going to the door and demanding to know who was there and what they wanted. Then we heard a voice say, "I have a package for Mrs. Moreland." I think we all screamed in unison, "Daddy!"

Daddy wasn't back long before his tragic accident. He didn't seem enamored with the US though. He was a man from a small town in a small country, and the big-city ways of New York City seemed to overwhelm him. He didn't like the trappings and excitement of the city. In his opinion, they would be bad influences. Plus, the cold winter weather did not do much to convince him otherwise.

We were a bit disappointed because we had our hopes set on going to America! Those hopes seemed dashed, and so we went on with the business of life as usual until the unthinkable happened. We thought Daddy would live forever. Yet here we were. Hope had only turned fifteen a few days before, and now Daddy was dead.

WHERE DO WE GO
FROM HERE?

CHAPTER 3

We buried Daddy a week or two after the accident. The funeral was an *event*. Friends and family came from far and wide. Some came out of the woodworks—we saw them for the first and last time. The celebration of his life lasted the entire weekend. Our family held the event in the city of his birth, in the hills, and included a Nine Night. A Nine Night is a traditional celebration. It is typically the culmination of nine days of celebrating the deceased, with the final and ninth night coming the evening before the actual church funeral services. A Nine Night celebration is typically not about grieving or sorrow. Instead, it is truly a celebration of life. The event includes a host of food, drinks, music, personal and cherished stories and memories, and games.

I remember Daddy's Nine Night celebration well, but not so much for the content as for my personal encounter. Eerily for me, that was the last time I interacted with him. Yes, I know he was dead by then. But my experience is my experience, and it was and is still very real to me. I was tired and went to lie down but quickly dozed off. The door of the room I was in was open; there was a light on and a chair in the hallway. I remember waking up because I heard a voice calling out to me. I looked out into the lighted hallway, and from my view, someone was sitting in the chair. It was Daddy! "Come here, come here, my little Martina," he said calmly and softly, using my middle name affectionately as he often would. "Okay, Daddy," I said sleepily, sitting up and slowly getting out of the bed and walking from the dark bedroom toward the light in the hallway. Before I could make my way out of the dark, I stubbed my toe against the footboard of the bed, fell to the ground, and was fully awakened. When I picked myself up, my toe was hurting, and my feelings were as well. I got up to run to Daddy, but there was just an empty chair as I entered the hallway. I heard the loud voices and realized the Nine Night was still ongoing, but Daddy was gone. Disappointed, I took my hurt toe and feelings back to bed. I was not about to breathe a word of it to anyone, as I already knew my sisters would think I made the entire thing up and laugh at me for years to come. (I can only imagine the teasing I will be subjected to when they read this. But I can take it now.)

With financial assistance from his siblings, Mother laid Daddy to rest in the cemetery at his family's church. Even now, if I close my eyes, I can envision the cemetery and the plot close to his beloved sister, mother, and father. Then there is the calmness of the small stream from the river that flowed through the area. As I recollect, it's as lovely as you could get for a burial site. It wasn't a cookie-cutter cemetery with hundreds and thousands of plots. It was small, private, unique, and unforgettable.

Mother cried a lot. Yes, she missed him, but I know she was also worried. What now? What next? She had been a housewife since she and Daddy were married. Daddy was her senior by more than one and a half decades. He was the breadwinner and the leader of the family. Now he was gone. She had a house with a mortgage, an old car (a Consul), less than $3,000 in the bank, and no life insurance. I could tell she was dealing with a lot. She didn't smile much, and she often had to go to a government office somewhere or the other to take care of required paperwork. Before this, I hardly ever remember Mother being away from home anytime during the week. I was used to her being there before I left for school and being there when I returned home. Now, I never knew from day to day when she had to go before I headed out to school and would not return until after I was home. At the time, I had no idea what she was doing. Still, as I matured, I realized there was a lot to do: filing documents, notifying agencies of death, and even trying to secure financial help (which never materialized).

If Daddy had left a life insurance policy, that would have been a big help. But that was not the case because Daddy had dealt with a bad experience and lost trust in insurance companies. When Hope was younger, Daddy signed up for a policy. The insurance policy included some educational savings benefits, which he thought would be a great way to prepare for her future. Well, the company went under, and Daddy lost his investment. Angry and stubborn as he was, Daddy declared he would never take out another insurance policy. He was a man of his word, so here we were now, Mother wailing because she did not know how she would make it with five children: Tina (Hope) fifteen, Regal (Champ) a few weeks from thirteen, Corrie (Faith) six months away from twelve, Kamere (Kam) six months away from eleven, and me (Sasha) four months after my eighth birthday.

I saw the sadness and concern on my mother's face. But other than Mother's outings to take care of paperwork during the week, the only change for me was that Daddy was not there anymore. I went to school and church. I read my books, listened to music, went out to play from time to time, and tried to get my chores done (usually with Faith's help). We ate dinner together, although Daddy's seat was empty. We never spoke about that change, especially not reporting about our day at school, reciting a poem, or giving a monologue on our career goals. We just went with the flow.

There was no worry for me. I had three square meals and a sweet treat now and then. From my perspective, there was no threat of homelessness, and Auntie Mattie was still sending boxes with clothing and trinkets for us. Based on my understanding, the sadness and concern on Mother's face were mainly about her missing Daddy. I didn't fully understand the economic pressures or her worry about our future. Again, I was eight years old, and my main focus was earning good grades. Anything else went way over my head. I certainly recognize now more than I did back then that life was not peaches and cream, but I am blessed that my mother made such a great effort to protect my innocence and allow me to treasure what I had and never feel as though I was less than or had less than others.

Additionally, I recollect the excitement when we took passport photos, and Mother obtained passports for each of us. It's hard to forget because it was during that time that we learned of the *Corrine vs. Corrie* debacle, as I detailed in the dysfunction of names. I was so excited about the mere possibility that one day I could get on an airplane that I think I looked at that passport every day. I cherished it, and I still do. I have the original document hidden away with my collectibles, but I pull it out now and then, look at that little girl and recall the memories with a big smile. It doesn't even bother me that I still get teased about that picture. It is precious and special to me.

Later in life, I realized that it was a totally different story for my mother. Of course, she missed her husband, but she was not only sad; in some ways, she was scared. She was not merely frightened for herself; she was even more terrified for us. Mother and Daddy had many plans and dreams for their five children, and when he died, she did not know how she could give us what we needed to take those dreams from hopes to reality.

As the months went by and Mother considered the situation, she knew what she had to do. She didn't have much, but she had a passport with a six-month visa—an invitation to visit her mother in the US. It was a big chance, but one Mother knew she had to take. She had to do this for her children, but she also needed to determine who would take care of us when she migrated—the answer to that question and the choice she made shaped our lives forever.

On another Sunday, Mother spent the entire day traveling to the countryside and back, but her trip did not produce the fruit she expected. She said she was beginning to think Sundays were bad news days!

"That day, I remember crying pretty much nonstop. I cried waiting on the bus, I cried during the bus ride, and I cried during my walk from the bus stop,"

Mother told me as we reminisced.

Mother's journey was one of great purpose. She went to the city where she'd grown up because Mother had a plan and a solution (or so she thought) to the question of who would take care of us when she was gone. Mother planned this trip to pick up a lady who had helped raise her and who had agreed to move in and take care of us when she left for New Jersey. Mother anticipated the arrangement would last a year or two. Other family members had done something similar, so she did not think it was an unreasonable request. She planned on paying her, and of course, Mother was covering room, board, and meals. They had discussed it and agreed on it. But, on the day that Mother went to get her, she was met with disappointment.

"I changed my mind. I don't want to do it," the lady told her unexpectedly.

Shocked, stunned, bewildered, Mother asked, "Why? What am I going to do?"

There was no response and no alternative offer. It did not matter how upset Mother was or how much she cried or even begged. Mother soon realized that no prodding or begging was going to change the response. Feeling beaten and helpless, she turned around and took the long ride home, changing several buses and walking to transfer from vehicle to vehicle.

That evening I stood at the edge of the driveway and peered down the street. I saw Mother walking home and alerted my siblings. We ran toward her and greeted her. She tried to smile, but it was in vain. We quickly saw the look in her eyes and noticed she was alone. I remember Mother trying to explain her concern about not having someone there to take care of us. Looking back, I don't think the younger kids (me and Kamere) understood the severity of what we were facing. Champ and Faith didn't seem to care; they were business as usual. Hope, though, fully understood and was clearly relieved. She had an opinion and lots to say.

"Well, I'm glad nobody is coming to stay here," Hope said to Mother unapologetically.

"Hope, how can I go now if nobody will take care

of my kids? How can we survive if I don't go?" Mother both asked and stated. "Your uncle is moving some thirty minutes away so he won't be down the street to look out for you children."

"I just turned fifteen, and I know what to do," continued Hope. "And, Champ, Faith, Kamere, and Sasha know what to do too. Of course, I will be in charge, and we'll live right here in this house that our daddy left for us. We'll go to school and do what we need to do. You go to America, work, send us money, and we'll get someone to come in just to cook and help us do laundry. That is all we'll need," said Hope, sounding convinced that she had a good plan.

Mother looked at her eldest daughter, sighed, and replied, "I don't know."

"Yes, you do. It's what we have to do because nobody wants to come here, and you're certainly not splitting us up. You will not send some of us to live with somebody and the rest to live with somebody else. I'm telling you now that's not happening," Hope replied adamantly.

"Hope, watch your mouth," responded Mother,

walking away.

I watched Mother walk to her bedroom, looking defeated. She didn't say it, but she knew that her choice was to leave or not leave. Mother also knew that there was no choice at this point if she was going to get on that airplane; she had to buy into Hope's plan. She lay on her bed, overcome with tears.

About a week later, on another Sunday—afternoon this time—we sat in the airport and watched the planes come and go. We had mixed emotions. Mother was leaving us, so there was sadness in our hearts, but the anticipation that this would mean one day we, too, would get on that airplane was exciting. Mother's tears told the story of her own emotions. None of us knew why these changes had come or why our lives had been disrupted. We did not know what was ahead for us either. What challenges would be facing us? Could we overcome them, or would we fail? I am not sure that any of us had the answers or a vision. I think we were in survival mode, figuring it out one day at a time.

Then we heard the announcement; they called

Mother's flight. She hugged and kissed each of us. She groaned, and her eyes were red and swollen as she cried profusely—and had been all day! But what I remember most is that she turned and looked back for each step she took as she walked toward the gate and the airplane. Without saying a word, the look on her face seemed to send the message—*Don't worry, it won't be too long. I will be back soon, and then you'll be able to come with me.* At least, I thought that was what she said as she looked back at us with tear-filled eyes.

As Mother boarded the plane and left for the US, I didn't cry. But then none of us kids did. It wasn't that we didn't care. In our innocence, we may not have fully understood the significance of what was happening, what we would have to deal with, and how these events would impact our lives. It's almost unexplainable, but we just knew what we had to do, and we knew that Mother would be back. Also, we felt deep inside that this was a step forward for us—for our future. Some said it was our innocence that explains it, and maybe they were right. I suppose it was optimism resulting from the convictions and beliefs our parents instilled in us. It was also the words we heard, recited, memorized, and carried deep inside from our Sunday treks to the local Anglican church, which we took dutifully—five youngsters walking together every Sunday morning, whether we wanted to or not.

Before you knew it, Mother was out of sight. Then we watched, smiles beaming as the plane took off in the sky. Our uncle drove us home and dropped us off. Our mother was off to a new life, and although we stayed behind, the same was oh so true for us. Things would never be the same from that day forward.

IS THIS HOW LIFE
IS SUPPOSED TO BE?

CHAPTER 4

For many years, I spoke extensively with Mother about her time away from us. Her stories have served as motivation and encouragement not merely to my siblings and me but now to subsequent generations. I kept her words in my head and my heart. I am finally documenting them, as I hope this story encourages someone along the way. Also, I am writing it to preserve the great memories and legacy of determination and perseverance that carried my mother through this season of disruption.

As Mother recalls, her arrival in the US was routine. She landed in New Jersey without much fanfare. At least it was still summertime, so initially, not having warm clothing was not an issue. She moved in with her mother and stepfather. It didn't take her long to find a job in domestic service. The immigrant network got the word out. There was an agency in New York City that could help.

One morning, after receiving this information, Mother took two buses and three trains in her quest for employment. When she arrived and entered the agency, the lobby seating area was filled to capacity. Looking around, Mother quickly noticed that most of the faces appeared similar to those of her culture and ethnicity and spoke with dialects that sounded pretty close to her own. They all had the same concerns, same issues, and the corresponding need—a job—to provide for family in a distant land. The lady at the desk asked Mother a few questions, reviewed her identifying documents, and directed her to a seat. I have heard comparable stories of agencies and experiences similar to my mother's from listening to her conversations with her network of family, friends, and acquaintances. Like my mother, many of these women were their families' lifeline, so they did whatever was needed to care for everyone.

Not long after her trip to the agency, Mother had a job. A family in Scarsdale, New York, hired her. Mother's new job was somewhat like her old job; she was hired to cook, clean, and take care of children in the household. Of course, unlike her former job, she took direction from her employers on taking care of their family, and these children were not her children. Still, she felt a sense of relief since she now had income. She needed the money. Her kids back home needed it. This was Mother's first step to achieving her ultimate goal of not merely providing immediate support for her family but acquiring opportunities that would allow them the future she and Daddy had planned for their children.

In her new position, Mother lived in a room in the couple's home. She could no longer live with Auntie Mattie and her family in New Jersey. Mother was on duty full time, although her employers allowed her one weekend off per month. On her weekends off, she headed back to New Jersey to her mother's house. She worked, saved, sent money home, and, of course, cried. She longed for the day when this would be behind her, and she would be back with her children and be able to give them all the things she dreamed. She trudged on from day to day, working hard and hoping for the best. Mother's life took on a new and arduous routine.

There were no vacations to exotic places, exciting, fun-filled weekends, or nights out on the town. No, there was not even an occasional meal from a carryout. Every penny Mother earned, she earmarked for paying bills, supporting her children, and saving for the future. Even clothing was scarce; she made do with the bare minimum requirements and humbly accepted hand-me-downs. Her lifestyle was not exactly geared to building self-esteem. However, she realized that this was not about her—it was about her children's future. Mother continued on her challenging journey without any complaints.

While Mother struggled with her new life, we marched on with our lives in clockwork fashion back home. We went to school, played with friends, stayed clear of trouble, and enjoyed the innocence that comes with youth. Each of us took responsibility for keeping up with our schoolwork, watching the company we kept, and helping at home. We carried on with life just as though Mother and Daddy were still there (for the most part).

Of course, like any group of siblings, we had our disagreements. Notably, the age-old battle of "you're not qualified to tell me what to do!" You see, Hope took her leadership role seriously, doling out instructions, coordinating the activities of the adults who did our laundry and cooked (including paying them from the money Mother sent home, which our uncle dropped off from week to week). Hope was not intimidated by the ages of the adults she hired. They had a job to do, and they had better do it, or they would hear from her, not just verbally but in the level of their wages.

Besides overseeing the general household support, Hope took pride in enforcing the family rules and reprimanding any sibling she thought stepped out of line or didn't carry his or her weight. While Kamere and I would dutifully obey Hope's rules and directions, that was not always true for the free-spirited Faith and the happy-go-lucky Champ. There were a few loud exchanges from time to time, but all in all, things went well.

Hope, who was in high school, traveled into the city by bus to school while the rest of us walked to school within the neighborhood. On a typical day, we arrived home before her. We knew the routine, put our school bags and books away, change out of our school uniforms, and complete our homework before Hope came home. Well, one day, I remember it rained heavily and flooded the streets. I am not sure whose bright idea it was, but there we were outside playing in the floodwaters.

When Hope arrived and saw us, soaked from head to toe, she was angry, to say the least. Kam and I were quick to run inside to dry off and clean up, knowing that we would endure some punishment and restriction. Not so for Faith and Champ; they were not backing down. In the end, after a heated exchange and Hope's threat to snatch a few of their treasured clothing items and restrict their treats, the two sides reached a truce. Like any disagreement amongst us (even today), it was over before you knew it, and we continue to laugh about it. I did enjoy stomping in the floodwaters, but I am sure happy they didn't carry me away.

We were not perfect kids. We were young, and we wanted to have fun. Even Hope wanted to have fun and enjoy her teenage years, and one way she did this was by throwing herself a sweet sixteen birthday party. Daddy always promised Hope that he would throw a big celebration on her sixteenth birthday. Sans our parents' actual presence to fulfill this promise, she made it come true independently. I always smile when I recall this treasured memory from my childhood. It was just about four months after I turned nine. We didn't have a birthday party or celebration for me or any of my siblings whose birthdays occurred before Hope's. But that was the norm. It was likely a factor of economics or a result of my parents' own experience growing up. We knew our birthdays, and we acknowledged each other's birthdays; but we never had a party, cake, or ice cream. We marked the new year ourselves, beaming with pride at being older, but without an official celebration.

Daddy's promise of a sixteenth birthday event for Hope was greatly anticipated by each of us, because if he threw a celebration for her, it was pretty likely that he would do the same for each of us when we reached this milestone age. So, we were in full support of Hope's effort to have an official celebration.

Hope's party was fun. And, though barely nine, I was there. Remember, Hope was never one to separate her siblings from each other for any reason. Plus, there were no babysitters, and she couldn't afford one even if she found one. I was home for the entire event and had the honor of bragging to my friends about the happenings at a party filled with teenagers dressed in early '70s gear (Hope wearing the new hot pants she had sewn for herself), darkened rooms, loud music blasting, and lots of chatter. There may have been much more than that going on. But, if it did, then it went right past my nine-year-old eyes and over my nine-year-old head. I know I enjoyed the music. I have always loved music—any kind of music.

Teenagers filled our house for the event. A few were from the neighborhood, but most were Hope's schoolmates who lived outside our area. I can't tell you how they made it there, but I can confirm they were there. The music went on for hours and was deafeningly loud. I am not sure whether we used the Grundig or if one of the young men brought their own equipment. Likely it was the latter. The Grundig was a big piece of furniture that we probably moved out of the way with the other pieces to make space for a dance floor.

After much dancing and loud music, finally, some adults came over to investigate what was going on at this typically quiet house. Eventually, they broke up the party and scattered the crowd. Again, I didn't get many details, but I think someone ratted Hope out to Mother. Mother sent Hope a stern warning through our uncle and an even greater reprimand in a letter. Ever strong and independent, the incident did not faze Hope. She felt she deserved her sweet sixteen party, and so she had it. She took her reprimand in stride and moved on.

I suspect that Mother did not take it lightly, but she was much too far away and still had too few resources or options to change the situation. I think after the messages and a stern letter, she did get
 one admonishing phone call with Hope (via our neighbor's phone). She then focused on her cause— getting past that six-month visa into a permanent solution and a path to get her children to the US with a plan for their future.

Her employers promised to sponsor her for a permanent resident visa (also known as a green card). But, as Mother tells it, as much as it seemed time was flying, the process of getting that green card seemed to crawl at a snail's pace. Worry, fear, and anxiety were slowly creeping into her thoughts. Mother was struggling to keep them from and taking over her psyche. Hope's little party certainly didn't bolster Mother's confidence that we would be all right living alone until she could move us to the US. But she had no other alternative, so she said she just continued working, crying, fighting off fear, praying, and hoping for an answer. Mother knew she needed a miracle, yet all she heard was silence. Day after day, she fought to hold on to her confidence because most days, she certainly felt that she was losing the battle.

From our point of view, we thought we were doing great, and things were going well. We were having a good time, still doing well in school, and we had enough to eat. Hope fired the cook because a few of her younger and more fussy siblings didn't like the meals. Hope took over the cooking chores in addition to remaining vigilant about her high school studies. She did retain help to do the laundry. This choice went over well with everyone involved. We continued our routines from day to day, patiently waiting for what was to come. We knew changes were ahead—Mother would never leave us alone forever. We just didn't know when things would change.

Hope started her last year of high school, so something had to give. She was way too bright, and both Daddy and Mother had big dreams for her and had instilled in her the desire to excel and reach for success. But there were not a lot of opportunities waiting for her after high school. Even as young as I was, I understood the concern. As I view it now, the bottom line is that we were heading to a crossroads, and someone needed to decide which direction to take. Still, we never discussed it. However, it weighed heavily on Mother's mind. Nevertheless, as we continued our routines, Mother continued her cycle: work, fight fear, pray, and wait for her miracle.

LOOK AND LISTEN, THEN STEP OUT

CHAPTER 5

Mother often talks about that time and her experience quickly adjusting to her new life, living and working in someone else's home, as best as she could. She says, "I did what I had to do." She went through her daily work routine and the once-a-month trip to her mother's home like clockwork. Still, she told us there were moments when she had to clench her teeth, fist, and everything else to deal with the situation.

In her regular world, children respected adults regardless of their title or position. I can attest to that. I would dare, oh double dare, one of us to step out of line or be disrespectful to an adult, and we would feel the wrath of our mother! There was no such thing in this new workplace. She took care of the house, and she took care of those kids, and they said whatever they wanted to her. She dared not respond. She wanted to, but she was smart enough to realize, at that time, that a response would most assuredly jeopardize the opportunities she dreamed of for *her* kids.

Therefore, as hard as it was, Mother persevered. She was patient, kind, and comforting to her employers and their extended family. She mastered the art of biting her lip to refrain from responding to the insults—specifically, those hurled at her about her culture and her country. She swallowed her anger at the comments made about her children, her physical appearance, and even her way of life. Mother was smart enough to know the mean-spirited slurs resulted from ignorance. She could react and get fired. But she wasn't inclined to do anything to throw off her plans and leave us shipwrecked. Mother chose to smile in public and scream in private, continuing her journey forward in this season of disruption. She was living what she taught us whenever we came home upset about being teased: "Sticks and stones will break your bones, but words will just bounce off you."

Mother looked forward to that single weekend each month when she headed to her mother's house. It was a chance to relax, eat what she wanted, spend time with her family, relish her culture, and find reasons to smile. The time between these visits grew more difficult, but Mother persevered because she knew it was necessary. At least, it was essential for right now. There were no other prospects on the horizon, and she had five children a world away whose hopes and dreams she carried daily on her shoulders.

While she said it took seemingly forever for each of her weekends in New Jersey at Auntie Mattie's to arrive, they flew by in the blink of an eye. Before she knew it, it was Sunday morning, and Mother was preparing to return to work. As she packed her things in a small suitcase, she dreaded the thought of taking the bus and train. The ride was long, and the wait was often even longer, especially when the season changed. The wind and cold were relentless. She bundled up as best as she could, preparing for her journey. Mother still tells us today about the biting cold she felt and the numbing pain in her fingers and toes as sometimes she stood for more than an hour waiting on a bus or train connection.

One particular Sunday (yes, another Sunday), Mother said goodbye to Auntie Mattie and the rest of her family, then headed to the bus stop to begin the journey back to Scarsdale after her weekend stay in New Jersey. Surprisingly, the bus arrived on time, and she was on her way. She transferred to a train for the next leg of her trip. Again, on this day, the wait at the train station was not too long, and the ride was uneventful. Still, Mother noted that it just seemed like an eerily quiet morning. Initially, she didn't think much of it, especially since it was one of those days when she wasn't feeling particularly sociable anyway. It was a frigid day, which heightened her sadness. She knew this wasn't good. Mother began whispering to herself, encouraging herself to take things one day at a time, believe, and cast out fear of the unknown. She tried to think of something to lift her spirits. Mother said she reminded herself that it would only be a few weeks until she returned for another weekend with her family in New Jersey. She hung onto this thought for encouragement.

But even the thought of an upcoming weekend in New Jersey did not stop her thoughts about her kids' welfare. She hoped we were doing as well as the letters said. She smiled as she thought, "At least I am sure they are warm." Mother prayed to God to continue keeping us safe. She said she asked God (as she usually did) to keep a band of angels watching over us, protecting us and covering us. It was about then that she heard the conductor's voice calling her train stop. She hurriedly collected her things and prepared to disembark.

She exited the train without incident. The station was empty and cold. "Cold, cold, cold. I feel like a prisoner of the cold. I can't seem to escape it!" she thought as she pulled her scarf closer around her neck and secured her hat. As she approached the exit leading to the bus stop, she noticed the station was desolate. There wasn't another passenger or anyone at all in her view. Before stepping outside into the cold, Mother remembers taking a deep breath. Then, she began the short walk to the stop where she would await the bus's arrival to take her on the last leg of her journey. She was doing what she had to do, but her thoughts and attention were elsewhere, hoping for a miracle to change her situation and that of her children. "It's a particularly quiet morning," she thought as she walked.

But on this quiet morning, Mother had an experience she never expected. She said she never noticed it until the last minute. Because her thoughts consumed her, Mother did not see the lone car behind her slowly approaching, from the same direction she was walking, and pulling up to the curb next to the bus stop. No, she had not noticed the car, not until the rear right passenger door opened, although the car was still moving, and a hand reached out toward her grabbing her coat. Instinctively she screamed and ran simultaneously.

Before she fully understood what was happening, she was in the middle of the street, attempting to get to the other side. She only realized she was standing in the roadway when she heard a car screech as the driver slammed the brakes, blew the horn, and shouted, "Lady, are you crazy?"

Mother said, "There I was in the middle of the street, my suitcase was on the ground, and my hands were on the hood of a taxicab." A cab had suddenly appeared just when she needed it. Within a second, she heard a car's engine accelerate, and as she glanced to her right, she saw the vehicle that had been pulling up to her at the bus stop speeding away. She laid on the hood of the taxicab, sobbing. The taxi driver put his car in park and came to her aid as he noticed her despair.

"They . . . they were going to pull me into that car," she said, her voice trembling with fear.

The taxi driver wiped his brow as he stared at her first with disbelief, but then, recognizing the fear in her voice and eyes, he picked up her suitcase and consoled her. "Come," he said, "I'll give you a ride."

"No, no!" Mother said, fearfully looking around.

"You want to stand out here by yourself?" he asked. "Aren't you afraid they'll come back?"

"I'll go back to the station," she answered.

"And then what?" he asked. "It's early morning, and no one's around. You'll miss the bus. Trust me; I won't hurt you. I won't," he said compassionately.

"Okay, okay. Thank you," Mother replied, crying.

Mother tells me she was confused and scared, but she had to make a choice. Something, intuition or instinct, told her to take her chances with the taxi driver. She got into the car. He drove her to her employer's home, and along the ride, she shared her story. Upon arriving at the house, she offered to pay him out of the little that she had. He would not take it.

"He was a blessing; an angel sent to protect me," Mother told me.

She asked God to send angels to watch over her children, and he was kind enough to send one to watch over her because he saw her need. Mother never saw the taxi driver again, but she remains forever grateful, always remembering him in her prayers even today. He paid it forward, and she doesn't doubt that he has received untold blessings.

Mother never reported the incident to her employers or the police; she didn't want to bring undue attention to her immigration status. This encounter increased her sense of urgency to find a solution for her challenging circumstances. She didn't know how she would do it, but Mother knew she had to make it happen. She had to find a new way. Things couldn't remain as they were. Her life and her children's future dictated the need for drastic measures. As she told me this story, Mother said to me, "I didn't have the answer, but I was more determined to find it. I told myself, Murna, you have to figure out this situation, and you have to do it quickly!" Mother was seeking a mechanism to initiate her own disruption of sorts to quell the explosion that had erupted in her life. Each time I reflect on this story, I wonder: *What would have happened if those men had successfully pulled her into that car? Would we have ever seen her again? What would have happened to us?*

SELF-DISRUPTION

CHAPTER 6

Days, weeks, and months passed. Seasons changed. The pages of the calendar turned without ceasing. The waiting game continued, and schoolwork was my primary focus. It was always important to me to perform well academically. Mother and Daddy's absence did not change my desire. Navigating the school system, complying with rules and mandates, understanding the grading system, and meeting expectations were not easy tasks for children left alone. But all in all, we made it through unscathed.

As I recollect, the school structure, class assignment methodology, and grading system were tricky. Uniforms were required, regardless of whether it was a private or public school. This requirement was a mandate. Any student who did not wear the defined uniform or whose attire was missing a required element of the dress code was subject to disciplinary action. For example, wearing white socks when your school required brown socks was cause for disciplinary action. In those days, discipline could range from corporal punishment (whipping) to suspension.

The uniform mandate in and of itself was a heavy lift. Skirts could not be shorter than a designated length outlined in the school's policy and rules. There were even requirements to starch and press seams and pleats to prevent wrinkles. Passing a teacher or administrator's inspection and complying with the uniform mandate was a challenge. Still, the classes and grading structure gave even greater cause to pause and wonder.

Each grade level included students grouped by A, B, C, and D streams. The A stream consisted of the students with the highest composite score from annual testing across all subject areas. The students with the next highest set of composite scores made up the B stream, then the next group the C stream, and the following the D stream. If a student in the A stream received one of the three lowest composite scores at the end of a school year, that student was re-assigned to the B stream of the next grade in the coming school year. For students in the B through D stream, those with composite scores in the top three at the end of a school year had the opportunity to move up a stream to the A, B, or C level (as appropriate) in the next grade. Those with the three lowest composite scores within their stream at the end of a school year moved to the next lower stream at their new grade level. Or if they were already in the D stream, they remained there. As unbelievable as this sounds, it was a regular practice. And it was also standard practice to post the grades, scores, and placements within streams on the wall of each classroom at the end of the school year. We knew each other's grades and class rank; it was public knowledge.

Daddy always impressed upon us the importance of performing at the highest level, so although there wasn't an adult present to direct us, we kept doing our part advancing in school and taking care of each other. Sometimes we argued, but mostly we took care of each other. We all did well in school with no worries about being demoted from the A stream. Most importantly, Hope graduated high school. Regardless of her parents' absence and no other adult family member actively involved enough to say "Job well done," she encouraged herself. We were proud of her, and we let her know.

As she always did, Hope pushed forward. She took college entrance exams, earned exceptional scores, and signed up for courses to stay ready for the next level—whatever it would be. We all believed more incredible things were ahead, even though we couldn't say what they were at that time. We didn't talk about it much, but we never doubted that we would have success opportunities. Daddy had firmly entrenched that within us before his passing. So, even though we didn't know what to call it at that age, we were walking and living by faith.

Mother, too, was holding on to her hopes and dreams for us. It was hard, but she believed. And, because she believed, she was determined to take whatever steps she thought necessary to bring those dreams to reality. But at that time, she said, her reality was one filled with despair. She was thousands of miles away from us in a different country on a distant continent. Her choices and steps were restricted, if not nonexistent, because she had no credentials to travel or pursue new job opportunities.

Her passport with the visa, now expired, was in the hands of her current employers, who had purported that they were working with attorneys to sponsor her to gain legal residence in the US. She had waited for more than a year, and nothing had changed. When she requested the status, her employer told her the government had placed a freeze on sponsorship. If she'd based her hope on that progress report, she would have given up. But her hope existed not of this world; instead, her hope was in promises God had placed in her and her husband's heart. She held on to her beliefs and stayed alert for directions. Mother hoped instructions would come soon because time seemed to be in a great, big hurry, yet solutions were not apparent.

On her monthly weekend trips to Auntie Mattie's home in New Jersey, Mother took the opportunity to talk to friends and relatives to keep her spirits up, get encouragement, and find motivation as she continued seeking answers. She chatted with relatives in Brooklyn and Washington, DC, and even spoke briefly with a few in Canada and London, England.

Mother told me of a particular occasion when her anxiety was through the roof. It was Saturday, and the following day she was scheduled to return to work. Her encounter with that suspicious vehicle and the taxicab remained at the forefront of her mind. Still, she knew there was no other choice but to return to work. She sighed as she gathered her belongings and prepared for departure on Sunday morning. Then she remembered her conversations with relatives and friends across the country and the globe throughout that weekend.

One exchange weighed heavily on her mind. It was a phone call with her uncle, who lived in Washington, DC. He worked for an embassy, and they granted diplomatic visas to his family. He encouraged her to come to DC and try her luck finding a job in an embassy.

"When the embassy hires you, they'll put you on a diplomatic visa. You won't have to worry about being an illegal alien and getting deported, which would ruin your children's chances to move here in the future," he told her.

"I don't know. I don't know if I should take that chance. These people I work for have my passport, and I am scared to ask for it. I fear it may raise suspicion. Plus, I don't want to mess things up if the sponsorship freeze ends and they can work on my papers," she replied.

"How long have they been working on your papers? I believe it's been over a year. You might wait forever if you stay!" he urgently coaxed her.

"I'll think about it. I don't know. I have to think

about it."

Mother thought about it for most of the day. Then something triggered in her. She knew she had to act on it. But she did not want to discuss it with anyone for fear that she would waver. She had to do it, and an idea of just how she could pull it off came to her mind. She had to take a chance and go to DC, and she knew how to do it. She jumped up, put on her shoes and coat, and grabbed her purse.

"Mamma, I'll be back in a few hours," she called out to Auntie Mattie, walking briskly to the front door.

"Where are you headed so suddenly, Murna?" Auntie Mattie asked, leaving the kitchen and following Mother to the front door.

"I won't be too long. I just need to get something," Mother replied, guarded.

"All right, be careful," was Auntie Mattie's response as she shrugged her shoulder and closed the front door behind Mother.

Mother said she headed out on her errand, smiling on the outside and nervous on the inside.

"I need to do this; I have to do this," she encouraged herself as she walked quickly down the street.

Within a couple of hours, she was back, opening the door to Auntie Mattie's house. Mother told me she had now replaced her anxiety with nervous excitement, but she was not ready to share it with anyone, so she took a deep breath and stifled her smile as she entered the house.

"Murna? Is that you?" Auntie Mattie called out, hearing the door open.

"Yes, it's me, Mamma," she answered, sniffling slightly and glad to be back inside and out of the chill.

"You okay?" asked Auntie Mattie, curious but never one to pry and prod.

"Oh, yes, I'm fine. I just had to pick up something I needed," Mother answered, making a beeline up the front stairs and quickly into the room she occupied on her visits.

She wanted everything to seem normal. She quickly put away her shoes and purse, and she hung her coat over the door as she usually did. Then she

111

went to the kitchen, made a cup of tea, and helped Auntie Mattie finish fixing dinner. Soon, the rest of the family poured into the kitchen, and they ate dinner. Mother excused herself early to finish putting her things together as she had an early trip in the morning to head back to work.

Before she knew it, dawn was breaking. Mother said the anticipation was welling up inside of her, so she didn't get much sleep. She jumped out of bed, showered, dressed, and gathered her things before making a small breakfast. Then she said her usual goodbyes and walked to the bus stop for the dreaded trip. This morning, she was alert but not anxious because she knew what action she needed to take, and she was fully aware of what was at stake. This plan was the road to her miracle, and she had to implement it, so she braced herself and got on the bus.

Mother was thankful that she arrived at her employer's home without incident. She rang the bell, and her employer greeted her as expected.

"Good morning, Murna! You are right on time. The baby needs changing and some attention. The kitchen is a mess," bellowed the lady of the house.

"Good morning, ma'am. Okay, let me get to it," Mother replied, dropping her bag in the corner of the hallway, quickly removing her coat, and hanging it on a hook. She went right to work without even an opportunity to change her clothes. Still, Mother remembers staying calm and keeping her composure by reminding herself how necessary this was—for right now. It was just a stop along the journey but indeed not the destination.

Mother told me she continued to clean, serve, and provide care all day. She finally got her bag and coat once she cleared the table and washed the dishes after dinner. After a great sigh of relief, Mother said, "I headed down to the basement to my small quarters, showered, prayed, and got in bed." She planned on initiating her plan in the morning. Tonight, she needed to rest and prepare.

The next morning, Mother was back at her routine, although she knew it would not be a typical day. She was up at the crack of dawn. She checked the laundry room and sorted the wash before heading to the kitchen to prepare breakfast for the family. Mother recalls reaching into the refrigerator to secure a tray of eggs when the lady of the house entered the kitchen. She knew this was her opportunity. They were alone. She had to seize the moment.

"Morning, Murna. I don't feel much like eggs this morning. Make some pancakes?" the lady of the house commanded while opening the cupboard and retrieving a glass.

Mother looked past her and answered in a somewhat distant tone, "Okay, ma'am, I will change gears."

"Is everything okay with you?" asked the lady.

Something inside her said, *Now, now say something*, Mother told me.

Mother responded cautiously to the lady of the house, "Yes, ma'am, everything is fine, but when you have some time today, I need about five minutes to speak with you."

"Oh, well, I have five minutes right now. What's your issue?" her boss asked curiously.

Mother said she then seized the moment, stuttering slightly, "No, no issue. Not an issue, ma'am." Then Mother continued as she washed her hands at the sink and dried them on a kitchen towel. "You see, ma'am, you know my kids are alone, and I've been missing them."

"Murna, you know I've been trying to get your immigration status straightened out, but it is not that simple," the lady interrupted.

Mother took a deep breath and continued meekly, "Oh, ma'am, I know. It's not you. I don't have an issue with you. But I need to see my children."

"Well, you know if you leave, you won't be able to come back because you have violated the rules. Your visa has long expired!" her employer responded threateningly.

"I know, ma'am. I know. But I still have to go. I have to go back. I know God will make a way for them and me. But I can't stay away from them any longer knowing they are by themselves," she answered, pleading to her employer. Then Mother continued, "So, I want to go home, and I need my passport back so I can go, ma'am."

"Well, when do you plan on going? And how do I know you will be going home to your country and not going to work for somebody else, maybe even right down the street?" the lady responded indignantly.

"I want to leave a week from today. I have a ticket already," Mother answered calmly.

"You have a what?" her employer asked angrily.

"I have a ticket for a one-way flight to go home on Monday. One way, ma'am. I know I can't come back, but I've made up my mind. I wouldn't pay for a one-way ticket if I were just going down the street to work. I can leave here on Sunday, go to my mother's house—my things there are packed already. Then Monday morning I will go to the airport and go home. I have a ticket, ma'am. I have a ticket—a one-way ticket."

Mother says that morning, she placed the ticket in the pocket of her work uniform because she expected these questions to come up. She reached in her pocket and produced the one-way ticket. The ticket was the item she purchased on her late Saturday errand during her weekend stay at Auntie Mattie's house.

The lady looked closely at the ticket and then back at Mother. "We'll talk some more," was all she said as she stretched her arm and returned the ticket to Mother.

"Ma'am, please, I have to go. I can't do this anymore, and I told them I'm coming home. You understand, ma'am, you are a mother." Mother told me she said it meekly and quietly as her voice cracked and tears streamed down her face. She was determined to use any means necessary to drum up some empathy from this lady to get what she wanted. "Please, please, all I want is to go home. I don't want trouble, and I don't want anything else," Mother wailed through tear-filled eyes as her body heaved.

The lady took a long look at Murna, her lips trembled, and her voice quivered as she replied, "Okay, okay, Murna. I will let my husband know, and you can have your passport—on Sunday before you leave. Please make sure you do everything I assign this week, especially since I must attempt to find a replacement quickly."

"Thank you, thank you. Ma'am, I thank you. I will do everything on your list. I want to get on that airplane. I thank you for understanding, ma'am." When Mother tells it, she notes that she was crying and smiling at the same time. Later that day, she quickly called Auntie Mattie to let her know she would be back on Sunday for a visit. It wasn't time for her regular once-a-month weekend stay, so she didn't want to surprise her family. She told Auntie Mattie that her employers were going away on an impromptu trip and did not need her services for a few days.

The week came and went without much incident. Mother made sure she went above and beyond. She smiled when she wanted to scream. She smiled when she wanted to hit somebody. She just smiled and hummed to herself. She was doing her part, and she knew God was doing his part, so she persevered.

Sunday came, and Mother packed her things. She

made breakfast for the family and waited in the kitchen to say her goodbyes. The kids said bye grudgingly, and then the lady of the house and her husband came in.

"Well, I guess you're really leaving us. What time is your flight tomorrow?" asked the husband.

"It's at eleven in the morning tomorrow," Mother answered.

"You still have that ticket?" he asked questioningly.

"Of course I do, sir." Mother said she wasn't shocked that he asked, but she stayed in character and allowed the scenario to play out as needed. She showed him the ticket. He looked at the front and the back as though he were inspecting it. Mother said she just remained calm and pleasant.

"Just checking that you didn't change your mind," he replied as he handed the ticket back to Mother.

"No. I didn't change my mind, sir. I just need my passport," Mother responded nervously.

The man reached into his pocket and handed her

the passport. Mother said there was great relief within her heart. She broke out in a big smile as she secured the document by placing it in her pocketbook as she said, " I appreciate it. And I thank you, sir. I thank you for everything."

"Well, we wish we could have kept you. But I guess you must do as your heart tells you. Have a safe trip, and we pray the future is bright for you and your children. By the way, this is for the last few weeks of work," he said as he handed her an envelope.

"Thank you very much," Mother replied without opening the envelope. They always paid in cash, and she wasn't inclined to check it this time. Although she needed the money, she needed her passport and the freedom to pursue opportunities much more. She quickly collected her things, and together they walked to the front door. She opened the door and stepped out. "Goodbye, and thank you again," are the last words Mother remembers uttering to them as she smiled and sucked the fresh air into her lungs, knowing the best was yet to come.

The couple barely mumbled, "Goodbye, Murna," as she stepped outside, and they closed the door.

Mother kept walking, never once looking back. She quickened her step, wanting to get out of sight and on the bus just in case they changed their minds. She made it to the bus and the train and then to Auntie Mattie's house in New Jersey without incident. Everyone was shocked as she told them her plan to go to DC. Until now, she had not shared her plans with anyone. Although it was a surprise, they understood why she'd left her job to take such a chance, because her most significant concern was for her children.

Mother called her uncle in DC to let him know she accepted his advice and would be there the next day. He, too, was surprised, albeit pleasantly so. He was looking forward to seeing her. And he reassured her that he would be there to pick her up at the bus station and make room for her at his family's home while she got on her feet.

The next day, Mother woke up, gathered her things, and said her goodbyes to Auntie Mattie and her other family members as she loaded her belongings into her stepfather's car. Mother said she was bubbling over with anticipation and wanted to leave New Jersey as quickly as she could because she still carried a tinge of fear that her employers were going to send the authorities to find her. After giving Auntie Mattie one last hug, Mother got in the car.

"Okay, Greyhound bus station next stop," said Pop-pop. "I know you're excited about trying your luck in DC."

Then Mother said, "I need to make one stop before Greyhound. We have enough time because the next bus doesn't leave until noon," she reassured him, seeing the confused look on his face.

"Where do you need to go?" he asked.

"The travel office. To trade in a ticket," Mother answered.

"Trade in a ticket? Are you okay? I thought you had a ticket for the bus?" he asked, confused.

"I have to buy a ticket for the bus. But I have to trade in this one-way ticket to Jamaica first," she said, laughing. "I need that money to buy my bus

122

ticket, and so I have some money when I get there. I have a place to stay, with my uncle, until I get set up, but I need to have my own money to eat and even pay them a little something," Mother explained to Pop-pop.

"Ha," he answered, smiling back but still not quite understanding.

Mother explained to Pop-pop how she bought the one-way ticket to Jamaica and showed it to her employers as proof that she was headed home so that they would relinquish her passport. But now she needed to return that ticket to get a refund. (Thank goodness in the 1970's trading in an airline ticket was straightforward and didn't require a fee.) She needed the money to help sustain her until she found a job in DC.

"You should have seen that lady's face when I showed her that one-way ticket to Jamaica," Mother continued sharing her story. "I guess she didn't think I could be smart enough to buy a ticket just to fake her out. Well, I did it! My children's future is hanging in the balance and staying at that job will not help me. I have a good feeling about Washington, DC. I heard about all the different embassies hiring. Now, I am determined to get work at an embassy and get a diplomatic visa—so I will be legal. I will not have to live scared and worried about that part of my life. And I think once I get settled, then maybe I can ask them for visas for my children." Mother was so happy she couldn't stop rambling about her expectations during the car ride.

"All right, simmer down. I know it'll work out, but don't get ahead of yourself," said Pop-pop, chuckling.

As the car pulled off, Mother waved to Auntie Mattie and threw her another kiss. Then she responded to Pop-pop, "I know, I know. But I can't lose sight of my dreams. I can't lose sight of my children's dreams."

That is the story of a season of disruption in the Moreland family and how we persevered. We didn't expect the tragedy of losing our daddy. We didn't expect our mother would have to leave us all alone to prepare a way for a better future. We didn't foresee the disruption and changes that threatened to overwhelm us. But our mother, who was not experienced in business and did not have formal training in handling disruptions, unwittingly embraced it and skillfully mastered it. She may not have known the standard steps, but Mother understood that taking a chance and trying something new would likely pave the road to opportunity for her children. Fueled by her faith and her will to persevere, Mother headed off to Washington, DC, to begin a new season; for sure, she knew the best was yet to come for her and us!

Mother never lost sight of her hopes and dreams for her children, and we didn't either. Throughout our lives, we've shared her beliefs, goals, experiences, and stories across the generations, instilling confidence in each other that tomorrow always holds real possibilities to fulfill dreams. Still, the bottom line is, you must be willing to set out on the journey.

EPILOGUE

My mother made it to Washington, DC, safely. Within a few weeks of her arrival, she found a job working in an ambassador's residence. Her employers granted her a diplomatic visa, securing her legal status in the US. Several months after receiving diplomatic status, my mother negotiated with her employers. They issued her diplomatic visas for two of her children.

After much consternation, my mother made the best decision she could. She used those visas to move Hope, a few months from turning eighteen, and me, who had just turned eleven, to the US. Mother said she made that choice because Hope had finished high school and needed the opportunity to get started on her next phase of life and carve out her path to success. I came with Hope because it didn't make sense to take Champ and leave her three youngest alone, and it also didn't make sense to take Faith and leave her youngest daughter with only young brothers to look after her.

She said, "It was heart-wrenching, but it was the

best that I could do."

Almost two years after Hope and I moved to the US, my mother secured three more diplomatic visas to reunite the family, bringing Champ, Faith, and Kamere to the US.

For many years, Mother worked tirelessly, sometimes holding down two or three jobs at a time to make ends meet and allow us opportunities she never had. My mother's efforts have never gone unnoticed in our family. We cherish her dedication and sacrifice, opening possibilities and enhancing our quality of life. She retired some years ago and can now enjoy the legacy she built.

Hope remains our fearless leader. She helped Mother guide us as we sought to find our way in our new country and community. Her siblings and the children of each succeeding generation revere her strength, integrity, commitment, and accomplishments. She is now retired after an outstanding business career during which she held executive leadership positions at a commercial real estate financing firm. She managed multiple departments and made significant contributions to critical strategic initiatives.

Regal (Champ) is still a fun-loving, likable man. Throughout the years, he reduced his participation in sports but picked up another passion, cooking. We all look forward to family occasions to taste his specialty, escoveitch fish. On the career side, he has supported a large member service organization for many years, developing expertise in their unique library collection and supervising junior staff members.

Faith is still our free-willed, no-stress sibling who we dubbed *the voice of reason* since she knows just what to say to resolve a disagreement. Daddy would be happy to see that she has had a successful career. She manages fulfillment, order processing (online, mail, and in-person), correspondence, and mail services for a major membership organization, guiding staff members handling a diverse inventory of products, and driving the organization's intake and reconciliation of significant revenue.

Kamere's focus on delivering on whatever he promised and remaining focused on the assignment at hand has served him well. He currently works as a project manager with a key government agency. Before his role with the government, he spent many years managing quality assurance efforts and staff for a private firm, overseeing a critical federal government contract.

Sasha never lost her love for books. She is still the family memory who can recall every event or activity from the past. Although she did not choose a career in teaching, she is the family tutor and mentor, helping several generations of children navigate their higher education goals. As for her career, Sasha spent several years directing product development efforts and managing notifications for large communications firms. In her current role, she supports reporting, risk management, and project documentation.

Over the years, our family encountered some tribulations, but we also experienced many triumphs; and the latter greatly outweighed the former. Our mother's legacy continues to thrive across generations. She has seen her children elevate their lives beyond her own and now watches as her grandchildren and great-grandchildren strive for and attain even greater success.

ABOUT THE AUTHOR

Through storytelling, we can share, teach, connect, and build relationships. As we share our stories, we inspire, entertain, and encourage others to learn, develop their talents, and explore opportunities. Likewise, when we read or listen to stories, we gain similar motivation, insight, and direction. I hope that my story inspires someone and encourages them to share their story.

My writing credits include publishing poems in various journals, self-publishing a poetry chapbook, *Mothers, Sisters, Friends*, and a collection of inspirational essays with accompanying poetry, *Lyrics of My Reality: Reflections & Inspirations.* I have also contributed articles to a motivational blog, everyday-power.com.

A Season of Disruption

www.writingsbyjackie.com

Made in United States
North Haven, CT
29 January 2023

31831513R00088